The
Germ Busters

Text and jacket illustration by

Rosemary Wells

Interior illustrations by

Jody Wheeler

VOLO

Hyperion Books for Children

New York

Copyright © 2002 by Rosemary Wells

Volo and the Volo colophon are trademarks of Disney Enterprises, Inc.

This book is set in 19/36 Bembo.
Printed in the United States of America
First Edition
1 3 5 7 9 10 8 6 4 2

Library of Congress Cataloging-in-Publication Data
Wells, Rosemary.
The germ busters / Rosemary Wells.—1st ed.
p.—cm.(Yoko and friends—school days)
Summary: When Yoko and her classmates become sick, Mrs. Jenkins comes up
with a great idea to identify who might be responsible for spreading germs.
ISBN 0-7868-0728-8 (hc) — ISBN 0-7868-1534-5 (pbk)
[1. Bacteria—Fiction. 2. Cleanliness—Fiction. 3. Sick—Fiction. 4. Schools—Fiction.
5. Animals—Fiction.] I. Title.
PZ7.W46843 Ge 2002
[E]—dc21
00-49906

Visit www.hyperionchildrensbooks.com

Mrs. Jenkins rang

the lunchtime bell.

"It's time to eat, boys and girls!"

said Mrs. Jenkins.

"What do we sing?"

3

The Clean Hands Song

(To the tune of "My Boyfriend's Back")

My right hand's clean,

and it smells like a daisy.

Clean hands! Clean, clean hands.

My left hand's clean,

in case you think I'm lazy.

Clean hands! Clean, clean hands.

We don't want germs

in a great big bunch,

Swarming and storming

all over our lunch,

So we cope with the soap

for a knockdown punch!

We've got clean, clean hands!

"My hands are so clean they

squeak in the air!" said Timothy.

Timothy unwrapped his sandwich.

"If a germ came near my hand,

it would die in the soap rays,"

said Yoko.

Yoko took a bite of

her California roll.

"My hands are the cleanest hands in Hand Land," said Fritz.

"How come?" asked Timothy.

"My mama is a nurse," answered Fritz.

"She brings Germ-Zapper soap from the hospital. It kills germs dead as doornails. I have seen it under my microscope."

The Frank twins dug into their

franks and beans.

The Franks had been

to the boys' room.

But they had not washed their hands.

They never did.

"That's for sissies!" said the Franks.

The Franks each ate their franks
and beans with one hand.
They each ate their Eskimo Pies
with the other.
"Good!" said the Franks.
"Good! Good! Good!"

"Those beans and Eskimo Pies

are covered with little hairy

hundred-leg germs,

blue with red spots!" said Fritz.

"Who cares?" said one Frank.

"You never wash your hands in

the boys' room," said Fritz.

"We don't care," said the other Frank.

"If you tell on us,

Mrs. J. won't like it."

Mrs. Jenkins rang the playtime bell.

The Franks wiped their noses

on their sleeves.

They never used tissues.

"That's for wussies!" said the Franks.

The Franks played snap-the-whip
with Nora, Charles, and Timothy.
Everyone wound up in a big heap.
Then they snapped the whip
again and again and again.

After playtime, everyone went
to wash up.
No one could tell if the Franks
had washed up or not.

On the bus home, Nora fell asleep.

Gus, the bus driver, had to wake

her up at her stop.

That evening, Nora did not

feel like eating her supper.

She went to bed early.

"You have a fever, Nora,"

said her mother.

All the next day, Nora stayed in bed.

That afternoon, her big sister, Kate,

came home from school early.

It was not long before their little

brother, Jack, felt sick, too.

Mrs. Jenkins telephoned

to find out what was the matter.

She did not like what she heard.

She thought about why everybody

was getting sick.

Her class washed their hands

before the "Clean Hands" song.

Didn't they? Everybody used

tissues. Didn't they?

Nobody spread germs.

Did they?

The next morning, Mrs. Jenkins
spoke to the class.

"Nora and her whole family are
very sick, boys and girls," she said.
"And now Charles, Yoko, and
Timothy are sick, too. Somebody
is not washing their hands!"

There was no answer.

"Somebody is being careless about wiping their nose on their tissue."

No one said a word.

"Somebody else knows who it is."

Nobody said a word.

"What happens when we tell on someone else?" asked Mrs. Jenkins.

"We're a tattletale," said everyone.

"And when is it important to tell?" asked Mrs. Jenkins.

"When telling helps, not hurts," said the class.

After school, Fritz whispered

to Mrs. Jenkins. "I know who it is,

but I can't tell," he said.

"I just can't do it."

"Well, perhaps you could tell

whoever it is to wash their hands

and use tissues to wipe their nose."

"It would not do any good,"

said Fritz.

"I will have to think of something

else," said Mrs. Jenkins.

"What you need," said Mr. Wagweed,

"is a Germostat. It sees the germs

for you. I could build one if I had

help."

"Our Fritz is awfully good

at science," said Mrs. Jenkins.

"We will try," said Mr. Wagweed.

Mr. Wagweed and Fritz worked

for hours, welding things to an old

TV screen.

"We've got a pretty good

Germostat, my friend,"

said Mr. Wagweed.

When everyone was well

and back in school again,

Mrs. Jenkins had something to say.

"Fritz and Grace have a new job,

boys and girls.

They are now the Germostat

monitors.

"Just before the Clean Hands
song, you must put your hands
under the Germostat.
No one may eat their lunch until
the Germostat says
they have clean hands."

The Franks snickered.
"They'll never find out with that
silly machine," they said.

"Ready, Fritz? Ready, Grace?"

asked Mrs. Jenkins.

Along came Nora,

out of the girls' room.

"Germ free!" said Grace.

Next, Charles put his hands under

the red light.

"Clean as a hound's tooth!"

said Grace.

The Germostat showed everybody

had washed their hands.

Then came the Franks.

They put their hands

under the special light.

"You can't see anything with that

dumb machine!" said the Franks.

"We know you made it all up."

Fritz pushed the red button.

Bing! Bing! Bing! Bing!

went the alarm.

Special marking powder shot out
all over the Franks' hands.
The red light blinked on and off.

"Germs!" said Grace. "Big nasty greenish-yellow germs! All over."

"Back you go, Franks," said Mrs. Jenkins.

The Franks had to try again.

But once again the light blinked,

the alarm dinged, and the marking

powder exploded.

"You can't see any germs on us,"

said the Franks.

"Come around and see," said Fritz.

The Franks looked at the TV
screen.

They saw germs of all colors.

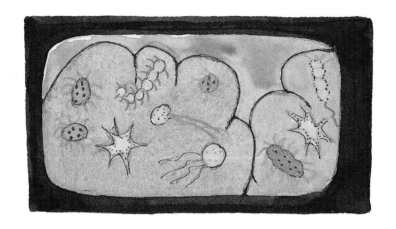

"Use soap this time,"

said Mrs. Jenkins.

So the Franks did.

"We will never not wash our

hands again," they said.

Fritz pushed the green button.

The Franks whispered about the

Germostat all day.

But they could not figure out how

it worked.

Dear Parents,

When our children were young we lived in a small house, but we always made a space just for books. When their dad or I would read a story out loud, the TV was always off—radio and music, too—because it intruded.

Soon this peaceful half hour of every day became like a little island vacation. Our children are lifetime readers now, with an endless curiosity for the rich world waiting between the covers of good books. It cost us nothing but time well spent and a library card.

This set of easy-to-read books is about the real nitty-gritty of elementary school. There are new friends, and bullies, too. There are germs and the "Clean Hands" song, new ways of painting pictures, learning music, telling the truth, gossiping, teasing, laughing, crying, separating from Mama, scary Halloweens, and secret valentines. The stories are all drawn from the experiences my children had in school.

It's my hope that these books will transport you and your children to a setting that's familiar, yet new, a place where you can explore the exciting new world of school together.

Rosemary Wells